Hodder Toddler

This book belongs to:

....

Flip and Flop

Dawn Apperley

Hodder
Children's
Books

A division of Hodder Headline Limited

'**Wheeeeee!**' said Flip,
'Look at me! I can stand on one leg.'
'Me too!' spluttered Flop. 'I can do it too!'

But he couldn't, and toppled slowly over into the snow.

Flip was five. Flop was two.
Whatever Flip did, Flop did too.

'I'm making a snow-penguin,' said Flip.
'Me too!' said Flop.

'I'm in my secret hideout,' said Flip.
'Me too,' said Flop.
In fact, whatever Flip did, Flop did too.

Flip and Flop played a made-up game
called Boomba. They jumped into
the snow, bouncing on their bottoms.
'Boomba!' shouted Flip.
'Boomba!' shouted Flop.

Flop loved playing Boomba with Flip.
He could play it forever . . .

. . . but sometimes Flip wanted
to play other games.

One day Flip was on the
play-slope, playing Slip-slide
with his friend Hip.
Flop waddled over.
'Play Boomba!' said Flop excitedly.

Flip loved Flop. Flop loved Flip.
But sometimes Flip thought his
brother was a bit of a pest.

'No!' said Flip. 'I want to play Slip-slide with Hip. Not Boomba with you. No way!'

Flop felt sad. He shuffled away.

Flop waddled and shuffled,
shuffled and waddled,
up and down,
round and round,
in and out . . .

. . . until he had wandered
far, far away from Flip.

Flop found a new play-slope and
started to play Boomba alone.
'Boomba,' shouted Flop and fell down.
He started to cry.
'Boomba is no fun on my own,'
sniffled Flop. 'It is boring and cold.'

At the top of the slope,
someone was watching him . . .

A little bear came sliding down.

'My name is Hop. Who are you?'
said the little bear.
'I'm Flop,' said Flop, grinning.
'Do you want to play Boomba with me?'
'Yes,' said Hop,
with a big, big grin.

Together they jumped into the snow,
bouncing on their bottoms.
'Boomba!' shouted Flop and Hop
as loudly as they could.
They were having a really good time.

'My brother didn't want to play
with me today,' said Flop.
'Mine didn't either,' said Hop.
'I'm happy I played with you,' said Flop.
'Me too,' said Hop.

Soon it was time to go home. The two friends skipped back to the play-slope.

At the play-slope Flip and Hip
were bored with playing Slip-slide.
They were looking glum.

'Flip, this is my friend Hop,'
said Flop, proudly.
'And he's my baby brother!' said Hip.
'Let's all play together,' said Flip.
'And make up a new game,' added Flop.

Flip, Flop, Hip and Hop invented
a new game called Slip-slide-boomba.
They whizzed, slipped, slid, jumped
and shouted:

'Boomba!' all together.

For Apostolos,
who makes me smile every day,
with love

Flip and Flop
By Dawn Apperley
British Cataloguing in Publication Data
A catalogue record of this book is available from the British Library.
ISBN 0 340 78799 6 (PB)

First PB edition published 2001
10 9 8 7 6 5 4 3 2 1

Published by Hodder Children's Books
a division of Hodder Headline Limited
338 Euston Road London NW1 3BH

Printed in Hong Kong

Goodbye
Hodder Toddler